D0883906

CALGARY PUBLIC LIBRARY

JAN - 2014

Copyright © 1996 by Verlag Friedrich Oetinger GmbH, Hamburg, Germany.
Text, characters, and illustrations copyright © 1996 by Lieve Baeten.
Copyright © 2001 by the Estate of Lieve Baeten, Zonhoven, Belgium.
First published in Germany under the title *Die kleine Hexe feiert Weihnachten.*
The original title in Flemish is *De kerstboom van Lotje.*
English translation copyright © 2013 by NorthSouth Books Inc., New York 10016.
Translated by Nicholas Miller.

All rights reserved.

No part of this book may be reproduced or utilized in any form or by any means, electronic or
mechanical, including photo-copying, recording, or any information storage and retrieval system,
without permission in writing from the publisher.

First published in the United States, Great Britain, Canada, Australia, and New Zealand in 2013
by NorthSouth Books, Inc., an imprint of NordSüd Verlag AG, CH-8005 Zürich, Switzerland.

Distributed in the United States by NorthSouth Books Inc., New York 10016.
Library of Congress Cataloging-in-Publication Data is available.
ISBN: 978-0-7358-4143-7 (trade edition)
Printed in China by Hung Hing Off-set Printing Co., Ltd. Manufactured in Shenzhen,
Guangong, June 2013.
1 3 5 7 9 · 10 8 6 4 2
www.northsouth.com

FSC
www.fsc.org
MIX
Papier aus ver-
antwortungsvollen
Quellen
FSC® C017606

Merry Christmas, Little Witch!

by Lieve Baeten

North
South

It was Christmas, and winter had brought with it a terrible cold, snowy wind.

"Come here, Kitty," said Lizzy the Little Witch. "It's time to decorate the Christmas tree. We must have the tree done before the Christmas Witch gets here and brings us presents."

Suddenly, there was knocking at the door.

Pound,

pound,

pound!

It was the Christmas Witch!

"Hello, Lizzy. I have a surprise for you," she said.

"Already?" asked Lizzy.

"Well . . . could you watch my little niece, Trixi?
I have so much to do today."

"Uh . . . sure," said Lizzy. She waved the little
witch inside. "Come on in, Trixi. You can
help decorate the Christmas tree."

But instead little Trixi wanted to practice flying.
Crash! Boxes of Christmas decorations fell all over the floor.
"Now I'll *never* finish," Lizzy said to herself out loud.

Just when little Trixi decided to help decorate the Christmas tree there was knocking at the window.

Pound, pound, pound!

"Ugh," shouted Lizzy. "I'm sure that's the Christmas Witch, and this Christmas tree is never going to be done!"

It was the Magic Bears!

Brrr!

"Hi, Lizzy. It's snowing so badly outside.
Could we come in and warm up quickly?"

"Uh . . . sure," said Lizzy. "Come on in.
You can play with little Trixi. I have so much to
do before the Christmas Witch comes back."

At last Lizzy could finally decorate the tree in peace. She was hanging bells on the tree when she heard *more* knocking.

Pound, pound, pound!

"Ugh," shouted Lizzy. "That's definitely going to be the Christmas Witch, and I haven't even started baking cookies!"

It was the Magic Vultures!

Brrr!

"Hi, Lizzy. We're freezing like icicles outside. Could we come in and warm up quickly?"

"Uh . . . sure," said Lizzy. "Come on in. Get comfy. If you play with little Trixi, I'll have time to bake cookies."

Soon the whole house smelled of delicious cookies.

"They're just about done," Lizzy said out loud to herself. "I'll have plenty of cookies for the Christmas Witch—and even cookies to decorate the Christmas tree."

Kitty wanted to taste a cookie so badly.

"Just a minute," said Lizzy, "they're still too hot."

Well, then. The Christmas tree was done.
Lizzy just needed a little magic to light it up.

"Hocus-pocus, with all of my might . . .
Give me a tree full of blinding light!"

"Oooooohhh . . . the magical lights are so
beautiful! And your tree, it smells so good."

"Come here," said Lizzy. "Come and eat.
These cookies are for everyone."

They sat together, so comfy and cozy, and nobody heard the Christmas Witch come inside.

"You have the *most* delicious cookies and the *most* beautiful Christmas tree, Lizzy," said the Christmas Witch. "And it was so sweet of you to look after Trixi. Thank you, a thousand times!"

When the guests left, it was practically morning. Lizzy waved good-bye to everyone, and at last she went to bed.

But, wait. Was that *more* knocking she heard?

The Christmas Witch had come back.

"Hello, Lizzy. I can't believe it," she said. "I'd almost forgotten your Christmas present!"

Lizzy beamed with joy.

Now her Christmas really was complete.